A Little Bit of Winter

Larson

ISBN 0-439-14783-2

12 11 10 9 8 7 6 5 4 3 2   9/9 0 1 2 3 4/0

Printed in the U.S.A.   24

First Scholastic printing, November 1999

A Little Bit of Winter

by Paul Stewart
pictures by Chris Riddell

SCHOLASTIC INC.

New York Toronto London Auckland Sydney
Mexico City New Delhi Hong Kong

Winter was coming.
"I'll miss you," said Rabbit.
"Will you miss me?"
"No," said Hedgehog.
"I'll miss you," said Rabbit.
"I know," said Hedgehog,
"you just told me."

"You are so forgetful," said Hedgehog.
"Forgetful?" said Rabbit.
"Yes," said Hedgehog.
"I already told you why I won't miss you."

"Remind me," said Rabbit.
"I will be asleep," said Hedgehog.
"You don't miss your friends when you're asleep."

Hedgehog picked up a little, sharp stone
and walked to the tree.
"Rabbit," he said,
"there's something I want you to do for me."
Rabbit ate a little green grass,
and then a dandelion leaf,
and then some clover.
Hedgehog wrote a message on the bark.

"I've written it down so you won't forget," said Hedgehog.
"Please save me a little bit of winter."
"But why?" said Rabbit.
"Because I want to know what winter *feels* like,"
said Hedgehog.

"Winter is hard and white,"
said Rabbit.
"Winter is cold."

"But what *is* cold?"
said Hedgehog.
"I am cold now.
Cold and . . . sle-e-e-e-py." He yawned.

Rabbit prodded his friend.
"Ouch," he cried.

"Rabbit," said Hedgehog.
"It's time for me to find
somewhere warm
to spend the winter."

Rabbit sucked his paw.
"I'll miss you," he said.

Winter was bad that year.
Snow fell. The lake turned to ice.
Rabbit was warm in his burrow,
but he was also hungry.

"That's the trouble with winter,"
said Rabbit, as he hopped outside.
"The colder it is, the more food
I want." He looked around.
"And the colder it is,
the less food I find."

There was no green grass.
There was no pink clover.

Rabbit had to make do with brown.

Brown leaves.

Brown bark.

A brown acorn.

Rabbit looked at the tree
where Hedgehog had written his message.
He dropped his acorn in surprise.

The acorn rolled.
It gathered snow.
It turned into a small snowball.

Rabbit read the message.
"Oh dear," he said. "A little bit of *what*?"
The wind blew, icy cold.
Rabbit looked down at the snowball,
and remembered.

"A little bit of *winter*," he said.

Rabbit rolled the snowball
over the snow.

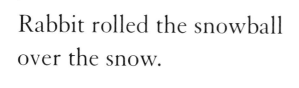

It grew bigger
and bigger.

Rabbit wrapped
the snowball in leaves.
"They will keep the warm out.
They will keep the cold in,"
said Rabbit.

"Then I'll store it
underground."

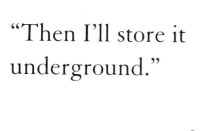

Spring finally came. The sun shone.
The snow melted and the lake
turned back to water.
Hedgehog woke up.

"Hedgehog!" said Rabbit.
"Rabbit!" said Hedgehog.

"Oh, Rabbit," said Hedgehog,
"you have eaten *winter*."

"No," said Rabbit. "I ate the bark.
But I saved winter.
It's in my burrow.
I'll go get it."

Hedgehog poked at the
soft, brown ball.

"You told me that winter was hard
and white," he said.
"And cold," he said.
"Just wait," said Rabbit.

He pulled off the leaves,
one by one.

Hedgehog stared at the snowball.
It looked like winter.

Hedgehog sniffed the snowball.
It smelled like winter.

Hedgehog grasped the snowball
in his paws.

"*Ouch*," he cried. "It *bit* me."

"*That*," said Rabbit,
"is what winter feels like."

"Thank you for remembering,"
said Hedgehog.
"I remembered because I missed you,"
said Rabbit. "Did you miss me?"
Hedgehog sighed.
"Oh, *Rabbit*," he said.